For Baltimore and DewMore
—B.S.M.

For Mama Winnie
—T-A.H.

HarperCollins Children's Books, a division of HarperCollins Publishers, 195 Broadway, New York, NY 10007

HarperCollins Publishers, Macken House, 39/40 Mayor Street Upper, Dublin 1, D01 C9W8, Ireland

A City Dream
Text copyright © 2025 by Bridget Sharise Moore
Illustrations copyright © 2025 by Trudi-Ann Hemans
All rights reserved. Manufactured in Capriate San Gervasio, Italy.
No part of this book may be used or reproduced in any manner whatsoever without written permission except in the case of brief quotations embodied in critical articles and reviews. Without limiting the exclusive rights of any author, contributor, or the publisher of this publication, any unauthorized use of this publication to train generative artificial intelligence (AI) technologies is expressly prohibited. HarperCollins also exercises their rights under Article 4(3) of the Digital Single Market Directive 2019/790 and expressly reserves this publication from the text and data mining exception.
harpercollins.com

Library of Congress Control Number: 2024942796
ISBN 978-0-06-326506-6

The artist used Adobe Photoshop to create the digital illustrations for this book.
Typography by Phil Caminiti and Honee Jang and Marisa Rother
25 26 27 28 29 RTLO 10 9 8 7 6 5 4 3 2 1

First Edition

A City Dream

wonder words by **B. Sharise Moore**   illuminating illustrations by **Trudi-Ann Hemans**

HARPER
An Imprint of HarperCollinsPublishers

My walk to school is a winding path of trash.
The concrete chokes the trees that help us breathe.
And I wish they would pause the sirens and hear our needs.

At school
we write about rights
and wrongs

and all the things we'd change.

My teacher asks how we will make our city great.

I'll walk to city hall.
I'll ask for more *murals*
and brilliant colors
on our walls.

I will sketch **playgrounds** stretching through the clouds, tiptoeing across the sky.

Ropes braided with hope on a swing that reaches the stars.

I'll outline my dreams to make sure **our water** always runs clean.

I'll hum to the soil, convince our food
to grow wild, wonderful, free.
I'll water the fruit and vegetable seeds.

Plant **gardens** on every block. Feed the people fresh food around the clock.

Teach my neighbors mindfulness.
Create *calm* when we disagree.

We'll go door to door and ask for helping hands.

Write **posters** and **poems** to protest the unfair laws.

But together we can shout our needs and write our change.

Plant our dreams and heal our pain.

I believe we can make our city a *fantastic* place.

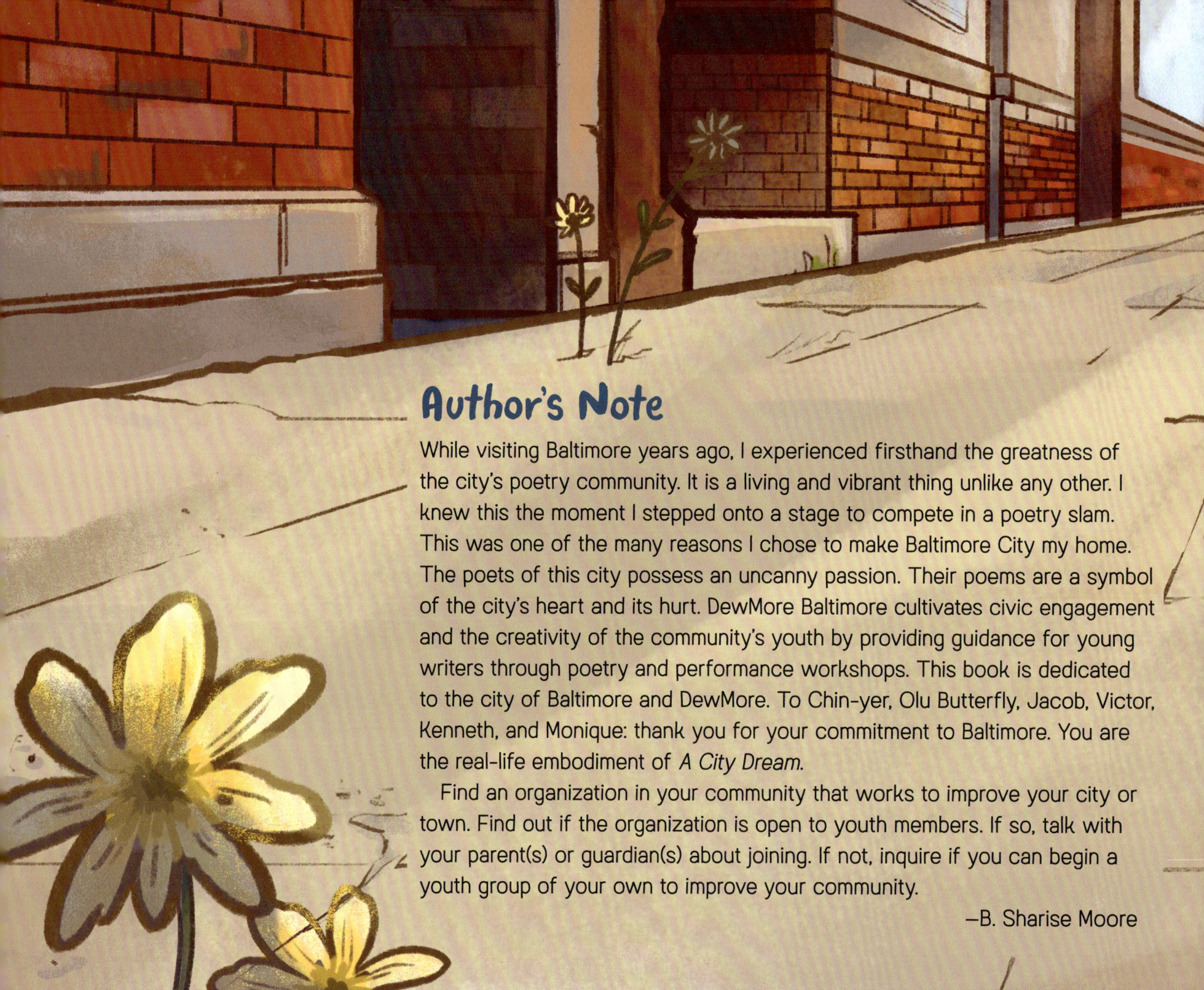

Author's Note

While visiting Baltimore years ago, I experienced firsthand the greatness of the city's poetry community. It is a living and vibrant thing unlike any other. I knew this the moment I stepped onto a stage to compete in a poetry slam. This was one of the many reasons I chose to make Baltimore City my home. The poets of this city possess an uncanny passion. Their poems are a symbol of the city's heart and its hurt. DewMore Baltimore cultivates civic engagement and the creativity of the community's youth by providing guidance for young writers through poetry and performance workshops. This book is dedicated to the city of Baltimore and DewMore. To Chin-yer, Olu Butterfly, Jacob, Victor, Kenneth, and Monique: thank you for your commitment to Baltimore. You are the real-life embodiment of *A City Dream*.

Find an organization in your community that works to improve your city or town. Find out if the organization is open to youth members. If so, talk with your parent(s) or guardian(s) about joining. If not, inquire if you can begin a youth group of your own to improve your community.

—B. Sharise Moore